Home Invasion

JOY FIELDING

Home Invasion

Grass Roots Press

First published in 2011 by Grass Roots Press

The Good Reads series is funded in part by the Government of Canada's Office of Literacy and Essential Skills.

Grass Roots Press also gratefully acknowledges the financial support for its publishing programs provided by the following agencies: the Government of Canada through the Canada Book Fund and the Government of Alberta through the Alberta Foundation for the Arts.

Grass Roots Press would also like to thank ABC Life Literacy Canada for their support. Good Reads® is used under licence from ABC Life Literacy Canada.

Library and Archives Canada Cataloguing in Publication

Fielding, Joy
    Home invasion / Joy Fielding.

(Good reads series)
ISBN 978-1-926583-31-0

    1. Readers for new literates. I. Title. II. Series: Good reads series (Edmonton, Alta.)

PS8561.I52H65 2011   428.6'2   C2011-902728-3

Printed and bound in Canada.

Distributed to libraries and educational and community organizations by
Grass Roots Press
www.grassrootsbooks.net

Distributed to retail outlets by
HarperCollins Canada Ltd.
www.harpercollins.ca

To Hayden

Chapter One

At first, she heard the noise as part of a dream.

Kathy Brown sighed and flipped from her right side to her left. Her hand brushed up against the warm body of her husband, Jack, asleep beside her. Kathy opened her eyes and stared at him. Jack's eyes were closed and his mouth was partly open. He was snoring. Even louder than usual, Kathy thought, trying to block out the sound. Jack's not doing it on purpose, she told herself. There's no point in being annoyed.

Kathy sighed again. Everything Jack did lately seemed to annoy her. Maybe that's what happened to couples after almost fourteen years of marriage. Or maybe not. Maybe something else was bothering her.

Kathy sighed a third time. She decided Jack's snoring was the noise that had wormed its way into her dream and woken her up. She sighed again — her fourth sigh in less than a minute — and flipped back onto her right side, so that she faced the wall.

Slowly, Kathy felt her body start to relax and her mind drift back to sleep. She hoped she could return to the dream she'd been having. The dream about Michael, her boyfriend in high school. He was tall and handsome and captain of the basketball team. She'd been crazy about Michael, and he broke her heart when he dumped her to go out with her best friend. Now, there he was, smack in the middle of her dream. He'd been just about to kiss her when the loud noise had startled her awake.

Falling asleep again, Kathy could not recover the soft kiss she hoped for. Instead, she found herself stuck in the middle of a dream about ants.

In her dream, Kathy stood in the large, all-white kitchen of her home in Maple Hill. She watched a parade of fat black ants march along the white counter. "Where did all these ants come from?" Kathy asked the young man standing beside her. She recognized him as the boy who had delivered her groceries a few days ago. The boy was tall and skinny, with chin-length black hair and a tattoo of a spider on the back of his left hand.

"There isn't much you can do to stop ants," the delivery boy told her. "They get in everywhere."

Then Kathy heard the noise again.

This time she opened her eyes and sat up in bed. She looked at the clock on her bedside table. It was two o'clock in the morning. The noise must be Jack's daughter, Lisa, coming home from her date, Kathy thought. It was an hour past Lisa's curfew, and she was probably trying to sneak in without her father finding out. At sixteen, Lisa was turning into more of a handful every day.

Kathy was about to lie back down when she remembered that Lisa was spending the night at a friend's house. So Lisa couldn't be the one Kathy thought she heard moving around downstairs.

Was there someone else in the house, or was she still dreaming?

Kathy sat very still for a few more seconds, on the alert for more sounds. But she heard nothing. Only silence.

"What are you doing?" Jack asked from beside her. He opened one eye and stared up at her from his pillow.

"Shh," Kathy whispered. "I thought I heard something."

"What?"

"I don't know."

"There's nothing," Jack said, tugging on her arm. "Go back to sleep."

Kathy lay back down. Jack's arm fell across her waist. His arm was heavy, and Kathy felt it weighing her down, like an anchor. Jack had put on weight in the years they'd been married. Not a lot. Maybe twenty pounds, most of it around his middle. To be sure, Jack was still a handsome man. His eyes were a deep forest green, and his lips were soft and quick to smile. At almost fifty, Jack still had a full head of light brown hair, even if it had started greying at the temples. At first, Kathy thought the grey made Jack look mature. Lately, she thought it just made him look old.

Not like her high school boyfriend. Michael still looked as good as the day he'd dumped her for her best friend. I never should have answered Michael's letter on Facebook, Kathy thought now. I never should have agreed to meet him for coffee. What's gotten into me? Kathy wondered. She hadn't seen Michael in more than twenty years. Why hadn't she told Michael that she was happily married and the stepmother of a sixteen-year-old girl? Or better yet, why hadn't she simply ignored Michael's letter?

Instead, Kathy had answered the letter and later agreed to meet Michael for coffee. And not just once, but twice. Then came Michael's emails, sometimes as many as six in a single day. And now here Michael was, in Kathy's thoughts and in her dreams, as real as if he were lying right beside her. Kathy pulled her husband's arm tighter around her. Maybe that way Jack could stop her from going to see Michael again.

"Mmm," Jack said. He snuggled closer and buried his nose in the back of Kathy's neck. "You smell good. Is that a new perfume?"

Kathy felt a sudden pang of guilt. She'd bought the perfume to wear for her meeting

11

with Michael that afternoon. She thought its scent would have worn off by now. "Yes," she answered. "Do you like it?"

"Very much. I like your hair, too. Did you have it done?"

"Yes," Kathy said. "This morning."

"Special occasion?" Jack asked.

"Not really," Kathy told him. She wished her husband would stop asking questions and go back to sleep. Did he suspect something? she wondered. "I was just too lazy to wash my hair myself."

"It's very nice. I meant to tell you earlier. I'm sorry," Jack said.

"No need to apologize." Kathy's hand moved to push away a few stray blond curls that had fallen across her mouth.

"I'm sorry," Jack said again.

Kathy understood that Jack was no longer talking about her hair.

"Do you want to talk about it?" Jack asked.

By "it," Kathy knew Jack meant the fight she'd had with his daughter, Lisa, at breakfast. "Not really," Kathy told him.

"I should have said something," Jack said anyway. "I should have taken your side."

Yes, you should have, Kathy thought. "It's okay," she said instead. "Lisa's your daughter. I know it's not easy for you." The whole thing is silly, Kathy thought. I've been that girl's stepmother since Lisa was two years old and she can still barely stand the sight of me.

Of course, Lisa's mother, Ruth, didn't make things any easier. Every time Kathy seemed to be getting closer to Lisa, Ruth butted in. Every time Kathy and Lisa started to form a real mother-daughter bond, Ruth made sure that didn't happen.

When Jack and Ruth divorced, Ruth had promised Jack that he could see Lisa whenever he wanted. The fact that she and Jack couldn't get along was no reason for Lisa to suffer, Ruth had said more than once. And for a while, she had been as good as her word.

And then Jack met Kathy.

And everything changed.

Ruth hated Kathy on sight. "She looks like a cheerleader, with her cute little nose and those big blue eyes," Ruth had sneered. "I don't think there's much room for a brain under all those blond curls." It didn't matter that Kathy had a degree in English from the University of Toronto or that she had a good job working for a major publishing firm.

Kathy's job meant she had to travel a lot, so she gave it up soon after she and Jack got married. "Kathy wasn't very good at her job," Ruth told Lisa. That was the first of many lies Ruth fed Lisa about Kathy. "She got fired."

For the next year, little Lisa had stared at Kathy as if she were afraid Kathy was about to burst into flames.

As the years went by, the lies got worse. Ruth did everything in her power to make sure that Lisa would never love her new stepmother. If Kathy bought Lisa a new dress, Ruth would tell Lisa that the dress made her look fat. If Kathy offered to pick Lisa up from school, Ruth would get to the school first. If Kathy got tickets for a play, Ruth would take Lisa to see it first.

"Don't worry," Jack told Kathy. "Soon Ruth will get tired of playing these games."

Except Ruth didn't get tired of playing games. If anything, she got even better at them.

"Things will improve as soon as Ruth meets someone else," Jack said. "You'll see."

Except Ruth never did meet anybody else. None of the men she'd dated since the divorce stayed around for very long. As the years went by, Ruth grew more and more bitter, and her dislike of Kathy grew stronger and stronger. Ruth spread that dislike to her daughter. By the time Lisa turned sixteen, she rarely spoke to Kathy unless Kathy spoke to her first. Sometimes not even then. Sometimes Lisa acted as if Kathy wasn't even in the same room.

To make matters worse, two months ago, Ruth got a new job and moved to Ottawa. Lisa had moved into her father's house in order to finish high school with her friends. Kathy had hoped that she and Lisa would now have a real chance to get to know each other better. But it hadn't worked out that way. Lisa still treated Kathy as if she didn't exist. Sometimes Kathy felt as if her home had been invaded by a hostile alien. At other times, Kathy felt her house now belonged to Jack and Lisa. "I'm the alien," Kathy said out loud.

"What?" Jack asked from beside her in bed. "Did you say something?"

"I'm thirsty," Kathy said, although she wasn't really thirsty at all. She got out of bed and walked across the hall to the bathroom. The bathroom tile was cold on her bare feet. She poured herself a glass of water. Then she stared at herself in the mirror above the sink. She wore a long white nightgown, and her blond hair fell around her shoulders in loose curls. Her skin was pale and her blue eyes sad. I look so tired, Kathy thought. Tired and old at forty-two.

Again, Kathy remembered her high school boyfriend, Michael. "You look so beautiful," he'd told her this afternoon. "You haven't changed a bit."

Kathy sighed again.

Then she heard the whispers.

This time Kathy knew she wasn't dreaming. She knew the sounds were real. She knew that someone else was in the house.

Kathy heard footsteps on the stairs. She listened as those footsteps grew louder, came closer. She stepped back into the hall. "Jack," she was about to call out when she felt something cold against the side of her head.

Even without looking, Kathy knew it was the barrel of a gun.

Chapter Two

"Don't do anything stupid and you won't get hurt," a man said. The man's voice was low and as cold as the metal of the gun pressing against Kathy's skin.

Despite the cold metal, beads of sweat broke out across Kathy's forehead. Her legs went weak, and her hands started to shake. She stared at the floor, afraid she was going to faint.

"Who are you?" Kathy asked. Her voice trembled. "What do you want?"

"Shut up," a second man ordered. A gloved hand pushed Kathy toward her bedroom with such force that she tripped over her feet. The man grabbed the back of her nightgown to keep her from falling flat on her face.

Kathy tried to make sense of what was happening. She told herself she was still dreaming, except her dream had turned into a nightmare. She tried to convince herself that there weren't really two strange men in her house. Men with mean voices. Men who were wearing dark woollen ski masks and black leather gloves. She tried to tell herself that these men didn't have guns pointed at her head and back. She closed her eyes and tried to pretend she was still asleep in her nice warm bed. Her husband's arms would keep her safe. But one of the men pushed her again, and Kathy knew she was wide awake. Her nightmare was real.

"Kathy," Jack called from the bedroom. "What's going on? Who are you talking to? Is Lisa home?"

Before Kathy could even think of an answer, she was pushed into the bedroom.

"What's happening?" Jack asked. He stretched to turn on the lamp beside the bed.

"Move and you're a dead man," one of the men warned.

Jack froze. He was wearing a grey T-shirt and a pair of old pyjama bottoms. Even with the lamp off, Kathy could see his face turn white with fear. "Kathy," Jack said, "are you all right?"

Tears ran down Kathy's cheeks. "I'm okay," she told him.

"Hey, that's enough chit-chat. Just do what we say and no one will get hurt. Sit down on the bed," one of the men told Kathy.

Kathy quickly sat down at the foot of the bed and lifted her eyes to the two strangers. Both men were tall. One was much thinner than his partner, but his arms had more muscles. Kathy thought that he must spend a lot of time at the gym, working out with weights.

The sound of the men's voices told her that both of them were young, maybe even teenagers. She wondered how they'd gotten inside the house. Lisa liked to sleep with her bedroom window open. Had the men come in through Lisa's open window?

"What are you staring at?" the thinner of the two men growled.

Kathy lowered her head. She didn't want to upset the men. They seemed angry enough as it was. They were probably very hot under those heavy woollen ski masks, too. Kathy wondered if they were also high on drugs.

The thin man pulled a piece of rope from his backpack and threw it at Jack. "Tie your wife's hands behind her back," the man ordered Jack.

"What? No," Jack said.

"You have a choice," the thin man said. He bit off each word as if he were chewing on a piece of raw meat. "Either you tie your wife up or I'll shoot her. It's up to you."

"No. Please don't hurt her," Jack begged. He moved quickly to Kathy's side and tied her hands behind her back as gently as he could. "I'm sorry," he whispered to her.

"Tighter," said the thin man. He waved his gun at Jack.

Jack tightened the rope around Kathy's wrists. "Are you okay?" he asked Kathy.

"Shut up," the thin man said. "Now turn around."

"What are you going to do?" Jack asked.

"Has anybody ever told you that you talk too much?" the thin man asked. He quickly tied Jack's hands behind his back. Then he made sure that the rope around Kathy's wrists was tied tightly enough. "Okay," the thin man said to his partner. "They aren't going anywhere."

There was something about the thin man's voice that was familiar, Kathy thought. Was it possible she knew this man? Who could he be?

Think, Kathy told herself. Who is this man? How do I know him?

"Okay. Just tell us where the safe is, and we'll be on our way," the thin man said. His partner began pacing back and forth in front of the bed.

"The safe?" Jack asked. "What are you talking about? We don't have a safe."

"Don't lie to me," the bigger man said. He suddenly raised his gun and slammed it against the side of Jack's face. Jack fell back against the bed, blood gushing from his head.

Kathy screamed.

The thin man slapped her, hard, across the mouth. "Shut up," he said.

Kathy saw blood pouring from the wound to Jack's head, and she started to cry. She was afraid he might be dead. Holding her breath, she watched for some sign that he was still alive.

Then Jack moaned. Thank God, she thought, wishing she could take Jack in her arms and comfort him. She glanced back at the two men.

They're going to kill us, she thought.

"Where is the safe?" the thin man asked again, seconds later.

"There is no safe," Kathy told him.

"Don't make us tear this house apart," the other man warned. He stopped his pacing and walked across the room to a painting of pink flowers. He knocked the painting to the floor and checked the wall behind it for a safe. But there was no safe behind the painting. There was no safe behind any of the other paintings that the two men ripped from the walls, either. Kathy could see the men's dark eyes narrowing in anger behind their masks.

"Where is the safe?" the thin man demanded again. His voice was even meaner than before.

Kathy lowered her head, afraid he was going to hit her again. "There is no safe," Kathy said. "I swear to you."

"Where do you keep your jewellery?" the thin man demanded.

"In the top drawer of the dresser," Kathy said.

The second man quickly walked to the dresser and pulled open its top drawer. The drawer was filled with Kathy's underwear. The man tossed the frilly bras and panties to the floor and pulled out Kathy's red leather jewellery box. He opened the box and emptied its contents onto the top of the dresser. "What's this garbage?" he snarled.

"It's all the jewellery I have," Kathy told him.

"It's garbage." The man spat on the floor in disgust. "Where's the good stuff?"

"That's all I have," Kathy insisted.

The thin man hit her again.

The slap stung the side of Kathy's mouth. She tasted blood.

"Don't mess with us, Mrs. Brown," the thin man warned. He raised his hand to strike her again.

How does he know my name? Kathy wondered. "My other jewellery is in the bank, in a safety deposit box," she said.

The thin man swore.

"Take her rings off," his partner said.

The thin man grabbed Kathy by the shoulders and spun her around. Then he pulled the rings off Kathy's fingers, tearing at her skin. First he took her diamond engagement ring, then her gold wedding band. He stuffed them into the side pocket of his jeans. Meanwhile, his partner went through the rest of the dresser drawers, dumping their contents on the floor. "There's nothing here but clothes," the man sneered. He stomped on Kathy's T-shirts and blouses. Then he marched from the room.

Moments later, Kathy heard the man moving around in Lisa's bedroom. Drawers opened and closed. Things crashed to the floor. Glass broke.

"What's going on?" Jack asked. Jack's voice was so weak that Kathy could barely make out what he was saying. Blood still dripped from the wound to Jack's head. He was as white as a ghost.

"My partner is getting angry," the thin man warned. "And it's not a good idea to get my partner angry."

"Jack, are you all right?" Kathy asked.

"Shut up," the thin man ordered. He slapped Kathy again.

"No!" Jack cried. "Please. If it's money you're after, my wallet is in the pocket of my pants."

"Hey, Steve," the thin man called to his partner. "Get back in here."

"Are you crazy?" the second man asked as he returned to Kathy and Jack's bedroom. "Now they know my name, you moron."

The thin man shrugged. "So what? They aren't going to tell anyone. Are you?" he asked Kathy, with a cruel smile.

Kathy shook her head. "No. We won't tell anyone. I promise."

"See? They won't tell anyone," the thin man said. "She promises." He laughed.

Kathy knew he didn't believe her. "I swear we won't tell anyone," she said again.

"Did you hear that?" the thin man asked Steve. "She swears they won't tell anyone."

Steve grabbed Kathy's chin. "Didn't your mother ever tell you it's not polite to swear?" he said. He turned to his partner. "Why did you call me back in here?" he asked.

The thin man pointed at Jack. "Man says his wallet is in his pants."

"Where's your pants, old man?" Steve asked.

Jack slowly pushed himself into a sitting position. He looked toward the small green velvet chair next to the window. "Hanging over the back of that chair."

Steve crossed the room in three quick steps. He grabbed Jack's pants from the back of the chair and began going through the pockets. Then he held up Jack's wallet. "Bingo," he said, dropping the pants to the floor. He opened the wallet and pulled out a small wad of twenty-dollar bills. "A hundred and forty bucks!" Steve shouted. "That's it? A hundred and forty lousy bucks?" Steve pointed his gun at Jack's head.

"I have money," Kathy cried.

"Well, now, what do you know?" the thin man said with a laugh. "Looks like the little lady has been holding out on us."

"Better tell us where it is," Steve said. "Or the old man gets it right between the eyes."

"The money is in my purse. In the den. Downstairs," Kathy said.

Steve stuffed Jack's wallet into the pocket of his pants. The thin man grabbed Kathy by the elbows and yanked her to her feet. "Lead the way," he said.

Chapter Three

Bookshelves lined the big, square den from floor to ceiling. On these shelves stood hundreds of books. Many of them were first editions that Kathy knew were worth a lot of money. She also knew that the men who had broken into her home had no interest in books. They only wanted cash and jewellery.

"Where's your purse?" the thin man demanded as he pushed Kathy into the den.

Kathy breathed deeply, trying to control the rapid beating of her heart. Her eyes shot from one end of the room to the other. She saw the comfy brown velvet sofa across from the large oak desk and its brown leather chair. Just yesterday morning she'd sat in that chair, writing an email to Michael, arranging their coffee date. A flash of panic shot through Kathy's body. Would the thieves take her computer? she wondered. Would these awful men stumble upon her emails? The thought made her feel sick to her stomach.

Kathy looked around the room for her purse, but she couldn't see it. Where had she put it?

Her eyes continued their frantic search. They raced across the pale blue carpet and the glass coffee table in front of the sofa. How many times had she yelled at Jack for putting his feet up on that coffee table when he was watching TV? Did these awful men plan on stealing the TV as well? How would they be able to carry it outside? Did they have a van waiting in the driveway to cart everything away? Were more men waiting outside to help them?

Kathy glanced from the desk to the window. Except for the street lights, it was dark outside. The moon was only a tiny sliver in the sky. There were no cars. It was the middle of the night, after all. Her neighbours were no doubt sound asleep. Were they dreaming about past lovers? Kathy wondered. Did they feel safe and snug in their beds, as she had only a short time ago?

Kathy doubted she'd ever feel truly safe again.

Somewhere behind her, Jack groaned. Kathy turned around just as Steve pushed Jack into the room. The front of Jack's T-shirt was drenched with blood. Red streaks marked his pale skin. He looked as if he might pass out again. "Jack," she said. "Are you all right?"

"He's a dead man if we don't see some money soon," the robber named Steve told her. He pushed Jack to the sofa and pressed his gun against Jack's head. His threat was real.

"I'm not seeing any purse," the thin man said.

"Maybe I left it in the kitchen," Kathy said quickly, trying to remember where she'd put it. Her heart was pounding. Her head was swimming. She could barely remember her own name.

"Don't play with us, lady," Steve said. "I'm not in the mood for games. Where's your purse?"

"I don't know," Kathy cried. "I always leave it on the floor beside the desk."

The thin man laughed. "Don't you know it's bad luck to leave a purse on the floor?" He laughed again. "My mother always says that."

Steve glared at his partner. "Oh, this is real good. Why don't we all just sit down and have a nice little chat? Let's get to know each other better," he said. "You can tell this nice lady all about yourself. And your mom. Maybe even the puppy you had when you were a kid. You'll make it real easy for the police to catch us later."

"What are you talking about? I wasn't..."

"Just shut up," Steve ordered. "The less you open your mouth, the better off we'll be."

"Hey," the thin man argued. "This was my idea, remember? You wouldn't even be here if it weren't for me. I'm the one who told you about this place."

What did he mean? Kathy wondered. Had he been in her house before? When? Did she know him? Her mind began to race. Where did she know the man from?

Could this young man be one of Lisa's friends? Could Lisa somehow be involved? Lisa was a smart girl, much smarter than either of these guys. Had Lisa planned everything, then stayed away during the actual break-in? Did she leave the young men to do the dirty work? Does Lisa hate me that much? Kathy wondered.

"Hey, who's the babe?" Steve asked suddenly. He lifted a framed picture of Jack's daughter from the desk. In the photo, Lisa looked relaxed and happy. Her brown hair fell to her waist, and she was smiling.

Lisa looks so pretty in that photo, Kathy thought. She tried to remember the last time she'd seen Lisa smile.

"Who is she?" Steve asked again.

"My stepdaughter," Kathy told him.

"Yeah? Where is she?"

"She's spending the night with a friend."

Steve laughed. "Is that what she told you?"

Kathy said nothing. What was Steve saying? That Lisa was lying?

"Too bad she's not here," Steve said. "We could have had a little party. Maybe we should stick around a while and wait for Lisa to come home."

"Just take what you want and get out of here," Jack said.

Steve took two quick strides back toward Jack. He raised his gun and pointed it at Jack's head. "What did you say, old man?"

"Please," Kathy pleaded. "He didn't mean it."

"You don't give the orders here, old man. I should shoot you right now," Steve said.

"There's my purse," Kathy cried. She saw it tucked away in the far corner of the room. The drapes almost hid it.

The thin man quickly scooped Kathy's purse off the floor and began looking inside it. Seconds later, he pulled out Kathy's wallet. He counted out three hundred dollars in crisp fifty- and twenty-dollar bills. He laughed. "Looks like she's richer than you are, old man."

"Big deal," Steve said. "A grand total of four hundred and forty dollars between them. Hardly worth the effort. What about credit cards?"

"Oh, she's got lots of those." The thin man took five credit cards from Kathy's wallet. "And best of all, a bank card." He waved Kathy's bank card in the air proudly, as if it were a flag. "This could be even better than a safe."

"You got a bank card, too, old man?" Steve pulled out Jack's wallet and peeked inside. "Why, yes, you do. Looks like we'll be needing your PIN numbers," he said.

"Don't even think of lying to us," the thin man warned. He grabbed a pen and a piece of paper off the desk. "What are your PINS?"

"7-8-7-0," Kathy said. The seventh day of the eighth month, 1970. Her birthday. "We use the same codes for all the cards," she said.

"Well, well. How nice of you. Isn't that nice of Mrs. Brown to make it so easy for us, Steve?" the thin man asked. He started to stuff Kathy's credit cards into the side pocket of his jeans.

"Better give those to me," Steve said.

"What for?"

"Might as well keep all the cards in the same place." Steve held out his hand.

The thin man slowly handed over Kathy's credit cards.

"The bank card, too."

"I thought I'd keep that one."

"Gimme it," Steve ordered.

"Why do you get to keep them?"

Kathy could see the thin man pouting behind his ski mask.

"Because I'm the one who's going to get the money, that's why," Steve said.

"And where am I going to be while you're out getting the money?" the thin man asked.

"You're going to be here, keeping an eye on these two. Once I get my hands on the money, I'll phone you." Steve looked at Kathy. "If everything goes smoothly, then nobody gets hurt. If anything goes wrong, then I'm coming back here to kill you both. Do you understand?"

Tears filled Kathy's eyes. She nodded.

"Tell me you understand," Steve said.

"I understand," Kathy said.

"I sure hope you do," Steve said. "But just in case you don't, I'm going to give you a sneak preview. Here's what's going to happen if anything goes wrong." Steve grabbed Jack by the front of his bloody T-shirt and pulled him off the sofa to his feet.

"No, please," Kathy cried as Steve brought his fist down hard across Jack's nose. Kathy heard a bone break. "No! Stop! Please stop!"

Then Steve slammed his fist into Jack's stomach.

"Stop," Kathy begged. "You're killing him."

"Trust me, I'm just getting started." Steve laughed as he let go of Jack and watched him slide to the floor. Jack coughed up blood and gasped for air. "I'm saving the good stuff till later," Steve said. Then he pushed Kathy to the floor beside her husband. Her knees hit the carpet with a thud.

Kathy wanted to cradle Jack's head in her lap. She wanted to wipe the blood from his face and kiss his broken nose. But her hands were tied behind her back, and all she could do was look at him and cry.

"Kathy," Jack moaned.

"I'm right here."

"Did they hurt you?"

"No, I'm okay," Kathy told him. "It's you..."

"I'm okay."

"How sweet," Steve sneered. "Sorry to break this up, lovebirds, but all good things must come to an end. Tie their ankles," he ordered his partner.

The thin man didn't move. "Who died and made you boss?" he asked.

"You want me to tie their ankles?" Steve said. "Fine. I'll tie their ankles."

Seconds later, Jack's and Kathy's ankles were tightly bound.

"We wouldn't want you running off anywhere," Steve said, and laughed again. Then he walked toward the hall. "Okay, I'm off. Why don't you check out the rest of the house while I'm gone?" he said to his partner. "I'm betting there's a safe here somewhere. And if these two give you any trouble at all," he added, waving his gun at Jack and Kathy, "shoot them."

Chapter Four

The thin man followed his partner into the hall. For a few seconds, the two men whispered together. Then Kathy heard the front door slam shut. A car started up and backed out of the driveway. Just then, the thin man popped his head around the den door.

"You got anything to eat?" he asked.

Was he serious? Kathy wondered. He was hungry?

"I'm starving," the thin man said. "How about fixing me a sandwich?"

"You want a sandwich?" Kathy repeated. Was this a joke?

"I know you have lots of tuna," the man said.

How does he know that? Kathy thought. Has he already looked through my kitchen cupboards? Or has he been here before?

The man didn't wait for Kathy to respond. He untied her feet and grabbed her by her arm. Despite his thin frame, he was very strong, Kathy noted. "Might as well make yourself useful while we wait," he snarled. Then he looked down at Jack, who was lying on the floor. Blood hid most of Jack's face.

All that blood looks like a mask, Kathy thought. She glanced from Jack's face to the face of the man in the ski mask.

"Don't so much as move a muscle, old man," the thin man warned Jack. "If you do, your wife is a dead woman."

Kathy felt a flash of anger. She didn't know which was worse, the threat or how the two men kept calling her husband an old man.

Then she flushed with shame. Hadn't she been thinking the same thing about Jack less than an hour ago?

Jack groaned, but he didn't move. The thin man pushed Kathy from the den into the hall.

Then he shoved her through the dining room into her modern, all-white kitchen. How does he know where the kitchen is? Kathy wondered.

"I'm going to untie your hands now," the man said, "so you can make me the sandwich. But I've got this gun pointed at your head. If you try anything funny, I'm going to shoot you. And then I'm going to shoot your husband," he warned. "Then I'm going to wait for pretty little Lisa. And when she comes home, I'm going to shoot her, too. Do you understand?"

"I understand."

"Good." The man tugged at the rope around Kathy's wrists. Soon Kathy could slip her hands free.

She rubbed her sore wrists. "Can we turn on a light?" she asked. She hoped the light would let a neighbour see into her kitchen. Seeing a man in a ski mask, the neighbour would surely call the police.

"Do you think I'm stupid?" the thin man asked. He pushed Kathy against the kitchen counter. "I want the sandwich on rye bread," he told her. "You must have some of that left."

How did the man know what kind of bread she had? Kathy wondered. When had he been here? Who was he?

"What are you waiting for?" the man asked.

Kathy pulled a tin of tuna from one of the cupboards. She opened it with the electric can opener that sat beside the toaster. Then she got the rye bread from the breadbox and some butter from the fridge. "I'll need to use a knife and fork to make the sandwich," Kathy told the man.

"Just don't do anything stupid," the man warned.

Kathy took a butter knife from the drawer and spread some butter on the bread. She thought of hurling the small knife at the thin man's head. In the next second she decided this was a bad idea. Her hands were shaking, and the knife wasn't sharp enough to hurt him. Kathy also knew she wasn't fast enough to outrun the man. She knew that if she tried anything, the man would kill her for sure.

And then he'd kill Jack.

And then he'd come back for Lisa.

And he'd kill Lisa, too.

The thin man smiled at Kathy. "You got any beer?" he asked.

"No," Kathy said.

"No?" the man repeated, as if he didn't believe her.

"No. My husband doesn't like beer."

The thin man laughed behind his ski mask. "I should shoot him just for that," he said.

"I have milk," Kathy offered.

"Milk?"

"Nice cold milk," Kathy said.

"Okay," the man said. "I guess I'll have a glass of nice cold milk with my sandwich." He plopped into one of the four chairs at the round glass table.

Kathy poured the man a tall glass of cold milk. She put the tuna sandwich on a plate, then put the plate and the glass of milk on the table in front of him. She couldn't imagine how he would eat and drink without taking off his ski mask.

"Sit down, Mrs. Brown," the man told her. "Keep me company."

How does he know my name? Kathy wondered. Who is he? Is he one of Lisa's friends?

Is that why he calls me by my last name? "I'd like to see if my husband is okay," she said.

"Your husband can wait. Trust me, he's not going anywhere. Sit down," the thin man said again. He patted the seat of the chair beside him, and Kathy sank into it.

The man tried to take a bite of his sandwich, but his ski mask got in the way. Bits of tuna stuck to the mask around his mouth and chin. "What are you looking at?" he snapped.

"Nothing," Kathy said. "I'm sorry."

"You think this is funny?"

Kathy could tell that the man was getting mad. She didn't want him to take his anger out on her and Jack. "No, of course not," she said.

The man grunted. He pushed up the bottom of his ski mask and pulled it away from his mouth. He had narrow lips, and one of his front teeth was chipped. She watched as he bit into the sandwich.

"I could use a drink," the man said as he chewed. "And I don't mean milk," he said as he reached for his glass. But his leather gloves were thick, and the glass of milk almost slipped from his hands. "Aw, the hell with it!" he swore. He ripped his gloves off and slapped them down on the glass table.

The first thing Kathy noticed was the man's long, thin fingers. The second thing she noticed was that his fingernails were chewed right down to the skin. The third thing she noticed was the spider tattoo on the back of his left hand.

Kathy gasped. Her eyes shot to the eyes of the man behind the ski mask.

"What?" the man said. He looked from his glass of milk to the back of his hand. "Are you afraid of spiders?"

There was a second of silence.

"You know who I am," the man said slowly. "Don't you?"

"No," Kathy lied, but it was too late.

They both knew the truth.

Kathy knew that the man in the ski mask was the same young man who'd delivered her groceries. That's how he knew her name. That's how he knew where her kitchen was. That's how he knew she had tuna and rye bread. He'd been in her house, in this very kitchen, just days ago. "Nice house," he'd said at the time. Had he made up his mind right then and there to come back and rob her?

"I don't know who you are," Kathy lied.

The young man laughed. "Then allow me to introduce myself," he said. He pulled off his ski mask. Straight black hair quickly fell around his chin. He scratched his nose, which was long and straight. Sweat dripped from his forehead into his dark eyes. He smiled, and Kathy wondered if his front tooth had been chipped in a fight. And how many other homes had he and Steve broken into in the middle of the night? "I'm Bobby," the young man said. "What's your first name, Mrs. Brown?"

"Kathy," Kathy whispered. She was sure Bobby could hear her heart pounding. What would happen to her and Jack now?

"Nice to meet you, Kathy," Bobby said. "You make a good sandwich." He took a big bite. "I noticed that you only buy the best."

"Please don't hurt us," Kathy said.

"Nobody's going to get hurt as long as we get what we want."

"Can't you just go and leave us alone? You have our bank cards..."

"As soon as I hear from my pal Steve. When he tells me everything's okay, I'll be on my way."

"My husband is bleeding. He needs a doctor."

"A little blood never hurt anybody," Bobby said. He took another bite of his sandwich. Then he drank half the glass of milk in one gulp.

He's only a boy, Kathy thought.

A boy with a gun, she thought in the next breath.

"Okay, play time is over," Bobby said. He stood up. "I'm afraid I'm going to have to tie you up again." He grabbed Kathy's arm and pulled her to her feet.

"No. Please don't," Kathy begged. "I promise I won't try to get away."

"Has anybody ever told you that you're a very bad liar, Mrs. Brown?" Bobby asked.

Kathy said nothing. He's wrong, she thought. I'm a very good liar.

She'd lied to Jack when he came home from work. When he'd asked her what she'd done today, she'd said, "Not much. I ran a bunch of errands, went for a walk, stopped for coffee."

She didn't tell her husband she'd stopped for coffee with an old boyfriend. She didn't mention how Michael's knees had brushed against hers under the small table. She didn't say anything about the touch of his hand. She didn't tell Jack that Michael's touch had made her heart flutter and her pulse race.

Okay, so maybe I didn't really lie, she thought. But I didn't tell the truth, either.

"Turn around," Bobby said now. He tied Kathy's hands behind her back much tighter than before.

"Ow. That hurts," Kathy said.

"Don't worry," Bobby told her. "It won't be for long." His cell phone rang. Bobby reached into his back pocket for it, then pressed the phone tight against his ear. "Hey, Steve," he said, glancing at Kathy. "I think we might have a problem."

Chapter Five

"She knows who I am," Bobby told Steve over the phone. He pushed Kathy back toward the den. "She saw the spider tattoo. What does it matter how she saw it? She saw it, and now she knows who I am."

Kathy tried to hear what Steve was saying, but she couldn't. Then she heard Steve laugh.

"Okay, yeah. Okay," Bobby said into the phone. "How's it going on your end? You get the money? Okay, yeah. Call me as soon as you're done. Then I'll take care of the rest." Bobby returned the cell phone to the back pocket of his jeans.

What did he mean by "take care of the rest"? Kathy wondered.

At that moment, she knew the men were going to kill her and Jack.

"Steve's got a few more stops to make," Bobby said. "He shouldn't be too much longer."

"Please don't hurt us," Kathy pleaded. How many times had she said the same thing tonight? Did she really think there was any chance that Bobby might not kill her and Jack? Once Steve called to say that he had all the money, Kathy knew that she and her husband were as good as dead.

"Just be a good little girl and do what you're told. Everything will be all right," Bobby said as they entered the den.

Jack hadn't moved. He was still lying on the floor, but he was no longer moaning. Kathy didn't know whether he was still alive. Bobby pushed her to the floor beside her husband. Only then could she hear Jack's breathing. "He sounds terrible," she said to Bobby. "He needs a doctor."

"He sounds fine to me," Bobby said. He began tying up Kathy's feet.

"Please," Kathy began again.

"Be quiet, Mrs. Brown," Bobby said. He gave her a mean look, a look that warned her not to say another word.

Once Kathy's feet were tied together, Bobby got up and began looking through the books on the shelves. "Looks as if you guys really like to read," he said. "Me, I like video games. You got any of those lying around?" He began looking through the drawers of the big oak desk, tossing their contents to the floor.

"Well, well. Look at what we have here." Bobby pulled out a bottle of whisky from the bottom drawer of the desk. "Looks like you've been holding out on me, Mrs. Brown." Bobby opened the bottle. "That wasn't very nice of you." He took one long swallow of whisky straight from the bottle, then another, and then another. "This is good stuff. No wonder you didn't want to share it." Bobby took an even longer swallow, gulping the whisky down the same way he'd gulped his milk.

"What else have you got in here?" Bobby began digging through the desk drawers again, tossing pens and papers to the blue carpet.

He doesn't care about the mess he's making, Kathy thought. He doesn't care about anything except the money.

She and Jack had to get out of there before Steve called again, Kathy knew. As soon as Steve phoned to say he had the money, Bobby would shoot them. Bobby might even wait until Steve got back and together they would finish off Kathy and Jack. Steve looked as if he would enjoy killing them both.

We have to get out of here now, Kathy thought. But how could they manage to get away? She was tied up, and Jack was barely breathing.

Kathy watched Bobby empty the last of the desk drawers. Then he sat down in the brown leather chair. The whisky bottle was now almost empty. Maybe if he got drunk, she thought, she might be able to convince him to let her and Jack go.

Bobby finished off what was left in the bottle. "You got any more of this stuff?" he asked. Then he threw the bottle at the wall, and it smashed into dozens of pieces. Bobby laughed. "Oops," he said.

Kathy took quick note of the slivers of glass lying on the floor. One big piece had bounced under the desk. If she could get to it, she might be able to use it to cut through the rope around her wrists. Then maybe she and Jack could try to escape. "There's a liquor cabinet in the dining room," Kathy told Bobby.

"Well, now, why didn't you say so before?" Bobby asked. He got up from the chair and walked into the hall. Bits of glass crunched beneath his feet.

Kathy saw that Bobby swayed a bit as he crossed the room. Was he drunk?

"I'm not drunk," Bobby told her, as if he could read her thoughts. "So don't go getting any stupid ideas."

As soon as Bobby left the room, Kathy crawled toward the desk. A piece of glass stuck into her bare arm. She bit her tongue to keep from crying out and kept moving. She quickly found the large piece of glass that had landed under the desk. Somehow she got it between her fingers.

Kathy heard Bobby moving around in the dining room. He opened the doors of the china cabinet. Sickened, she heard her good china breaking as Bobby flung cups and saucers to the floor. How long would he take to find the liquor cabinet? She didn't have much time left. She had to work fast.

Bits of glass stuck to Kathy's cotton nightgown as she crawled back to Jack's side. "We're going to get out of here," she told him, but he didn't respond. "Hang on, sweetheart," she said. "Please hang on." She tried to get the piece of glass in her fingers into the right position to cut through the rope, but the glass kept slipping. "Oh, no," she cried as the glass fell to the floor. Her eyes searched for it on the blue carpet around her.

Kathy could still hear Bobby in the dining room. "Come out, come out, wherever you are," he said. For a minute she thought Bobby was talking to her, and she froze. Then she realized he was talking to the whisky he hoped to find.

Kathy twisted around, looking for the lost piece of glass. "Where are you?" she cried softly.

"Come out, come out, wherever you are," Bobby called out again.

"Come out, come out, wherever you are," she whispered along with him.

"There you are," Bobby said.

"There you are." Kathy saw the piece of glass. Slowly and carefully, she managed to get it back between her fingers.

Just then, Bobby returned to the den. He was holding a brand new bottle of malt whisky. "Look what I found," he said. He plopped down on the sofa and lifted his feet to the glass coffee table. He was wearing heavy black boots with pointed toes. The bottoms were covered with dried mud. "I'm afraid I made a bit of a mess in the dining room," Bobby said, and laughed.

He tried to open the whisky bottle, but his hands were too shaky. The bottle cap wouldn't budge. "What's the matter with this stupid thing?" he asked. Kathy could hear the growing anger in his voice. "Can you open this stupid thing?" Bobby asked her. He lowered his feet to the floor.

Kathy held her breath. Was Bobby planning to untie her hands so she could open the bottle? If he came over, he would see the piece of glass hidden in her palm. And then what? Would he be so angry that he'd use it to slash her throat?

Kathy gripped the piece of broken glass tighter in the palm of her hand. Maybe Bobby wouldn't notice it. And if he did notice it, could Kathy use it on him? Was she capable of harming another human being?

A few days ago, Kathy would have answered "no" to both questions. She'd always been such a good girl. The child who always did as she was told. The teenager who always had her homework done. Kathy had never given her parents any real trouble. She'd always followed the rules. Kathy wasn't a risk taker. She wasn't a rule breaker.

And yet, the last few days had changed all that. Since Michael had looked her up on Facebook, Kathy had turned into someone she barely knew. She'd become a woman who kept secrets. She'd become a woman who snuck around and did things behind her husband's back. How had she let that happen? How had she allowed Michael, who had caused her so much pain, to invade her life again?

Kathy held her breath as Bobby pushed himself off the sofa. Then he suddenly sank back down. "Well, what do you know?" Bobby said. "The cap came off." He laughed as he threw the bottle cap to the floor. Then he put his dirty boots back up on the coffee table. He took a long drink of the whisky. "That's better," he said with a smile. "Much, much better."

Kathy sighed with relief. As long as Bobby kept drinking, she might have a chance. She might cut through the rope that bound her wrists behind her back. She and Jack might have a chance of getting out of the house alive.

Kathy could see that her husband was badly hurt. Jack's breathing was as jagged as the piece of glass between her fingers. "I love you," she whispered to him.

"Did you say something?" Bobby asked. He was staring at the floor.

Again Kathy held her breath. Had Bobby noticed the broken glass on the carpet? Had he figured out what she was up to?

Bobby lifted his feet off the table and stretched out on the sofa. He laid his head against one of the sofa's soft brown pillows and took another sip from the whisky bottle. He closed his eyes. "I'm watching you," he said.

Was he? Kathy wondered. Or was he about to pass out from all the liquor he'd been drinking?

Kathy began gently rubbing the piece of glass in her hands against the rope. Back and forth, back and forth. Soon gentle snoring came from the sofa. Seconds later, the almost-empty bottle slipped from Bobby's hands and fell to the floor.

Chapter Six

Kathy waited until she was sure that Bobby was asleep. Then she pushed herself onto her knees. "Bobby," she called softly. Then again, a little louder, "Bobby!"

Bobby said nothing.

"Bobby," Kathy called a third time. She wondered if Bobby was really asleep or if he was just playing with her.

Bobby snored again.

I don't have much time, Kathy thought. I have to move fast. Bobby might not sleep for long. Steve would phone any minute to tell Bobby he had the money. It would be Bobby's turn to "take care of the rest."

Kathy tried harder to cut through the rope at her wrists, but she had no luck. She kept losing her grip on the glass. "It's not working," she cried. "I can't do this."

Bobby flipped over onto his side. Now he faced her. Are his eyes open? Kathy wondered. Does he know what I'm doing? Does he think this is funny? Kathy stared through the darkness. She was afraid to move.

She sat still until she knew for sure that Bobby was asleep. Then she tried again to cut through the rope. But her hands were shaking. Once again, the glass slipped, cutting into her skin instead of the rope. Kathy cried out in pain as she dropped the glass.

Bobby stirred with the sound of her cry, but he didn't wake up.

I'm so stupid, Kathy moaned. No wonder my stepdaughter hates me. Lisa thinks I'm stupid and silly and not worth her time. And Lisa is right. I'm useless. I can't do anything. No wonder Lisa hates me.

Guilt suddenly stabbed her. When the two masked men had grabbed her in the hall, Kathy's first thought had been to blame Lisa. Steve and Bobby had likely got into the house through Lisa's open window. She had felt pretty sure that the men were friends of Lisa's. For a few seconds, Kathy had even wondered whether Lisa might be the brains behind this home invasion.

And all the time, it was my fault, Kathy thought now. I'm the one who let Bobby inside the house when he delivered my groceries. Kathy remembered leading Bobby through the front hall and dining room into the kitchen. She'd told him to put the groceries on the counter. She said she liked the spider tattoo on the back of his hand, even though she really found it creepy. Bobby, in turn, had pointed out the ants, just as he had in her dream. He even gave her the name of a product that would get rid of the ants. "Nice house," Bobby had said before he left.

At the time, Kathy thought he was a very sweet young man. Which just goes to show what a great judge of people I am, Kathy thought now.

She pictured Michael. Hadn't she once thought Michael was very sweet, too? In high school, she'd been crazy about him, bragging about their great love to all her friends. And then he'd dumped her without warning for one of those friends. What a jerk Michael had turned out to be.

And yet I answered Michael's emails, Kathy thought. I met him for coffee, not once, but twice. After all these years, I let him steal back into my mind and my heart and my life. Why? Because Michael is handsome and charming and I'm restless and a little bored? Because I'm tired of trying to win over my stepdaughter and want to return to a time when life was easy?

When had life ever been easy?

I don't want Michael, Kathy now understood.

I want my husband.

I love Jack and the life we've built together, Kathy thought. How could I have risked losing it?

Kathy glanced at her husband, who lay on the floor in a pool of his own blood. Please don't die, she prayed silently. Please let us get out of here before Bobby wakes up and Steve comes back.

Kathy searched the carpet with her eyes for the piece of glass she'd dropped. Finally she found it. Once more, she gripped it between her bleeding fingers, then began rubbing it back and forth across the rope. If she could just free her hands, then she could untie her feet. And then she could untie Jack, and together they could make their escape.

All at once, Kathy heard a pop and felt the rope snap.

Her hands were free.

Kathy moved quickly to untie her feet. "Jack," she whispered. "Jack, wake up."

A sudden noise made her look up. She feared seeing Bobby standing there with his gun pointed at her head. But Bobby was still sound asleep on the sofa, his gun resting in his hand. Can I get that gun out of his hand without waking him up? Kathy wondered.

Just get out of here, she decided. Again she tried to wake up Jack. "Jack, Jack, darling. Please, can you hear me?"

Jack moaned and opened his eyes. "What's happening?"

"Shh," Kathy warned as she kissed Jack's cheek. "Listen to me. The man fell asleep." She started to untie Jack's feet. "We have to get out of here before he wakes up. Do you understand?"

"I don't think I can move," Jack said. "I think my ribs might be broken." His voice was so quiet Kathy could barely hear him.

"You have to get up," Kathy whispered. "If we don't get out of here, these men will kill us."

"You go," Jack said. "Go without me."

"No way," Kathy told him. "Can you try to sit up?"

Jack groaned and pushed himself into a sitting position. Kathy reached behind his back and untied the rope at his wrists. Then she grabbed Jack beneath his arms and tried to pull him to his feet. Jack let out a sharp cry of pain.

Kathy's eyes shot to Bobby. Had he heard Jack's cry?

Bobby flipped onto his back, as if he might be waking up. But in the next second, he settled back into sleep. Kathy saw that his gun was still in his hand.

Could she get it?

Could she use it?

"I don't think I can do this," Jack said.

Kathy looked around. She tried to figure out her next move. Then she remembered her purse. It was on the floor beside the sofa, near Bobby's head. My cell phone is inside that purse, Kathy thought.

If she could get to it, she might be able to call 9-1-1.

Kathy gently took her arms away from Jack and pushed herself to her feet. She tiptoed across the carpet to where her purse lay. Slowly she reached for it. Just then Bobby let out a loud snore and Kathy jumped. She grabbed her purse and returned quickly to Jack's side. Then she reached inside the purse and pulled out her cell phone.

Kathy opened the phone and pressed 9-1-1. After several rings, someone answered. "I'm the victim of a home invasion," Kathy whispered to the voice on the other end. "Please help me."

"I'm sorry, ma'am," the woman on the other end said. "I can't hear you. You'll have to speak up."

"I can't," Kathy said, as loudly as she could. She gave the woman her home address. "My home has been broken into," she said, as Bobby stirred on the sofa. "Please, send the police. Hurry."

"Just leave me here," Jack urged. "Please. Just go."

"I'm not going anywhere without you," Kathy said. Again she tried to lift Jack up. Again she failed. "You have to help me, Jack. I know it's hard. I know it hurts. But you have to help me."

Jack took a deep breath, pushed himself to his feet, and grabbed hold of Kathy. His body leaning into hers, they took the smallest of baby steps. The short walk to the hall felt like an endless journey. Would they ever make it?

Kathy pictured Bobby waking up and coming after them. Would Bobby yell at them to stop? Or would he simply shoot them in the back as they tried to flee? Would the police get here in time? Had the woman at 9-1-1 understood the address Kathy gave her? Did she understand that lives were at stake?

"Almost there," Kathy whispered to Jack. They hurried as best they could across the hall to the front door. "Just a few more steps."

They were almost at the front door when Bobby's cell phone rang.

"No, please, no," Kathy prayed. Her hand stretched toward the doorknob.

Bobby's phone kept ringing. How long before the sound reached inside his brain and shook him awake? How long before he opened his eyes? How long before he realized that Kathy and Jack were no longer in the room? How long before he came running after them?

Kathy's fingers wrapped around the doorknob. At the same instant, Bobby's phone stopped ringing.

"Hello," Bobby said.

Kathy pictured Bobby sitting up and wiping the sleep from his eyes. She pictured him looking around the den. She pictured him peering through the darkness. She pictured him trying to make sense of what he saw. She pictured his panic when he realized she and Jack were gone.

"Are you ready?" Kathy asked her husband. Her fingers gripped the doorknob.

Jack nodded.

Kathy pulled open the door, and she and Jack stepped into the night.

And then everything seemed to happen at once.

In the cool night air, Kathy dragged Jack toward the road. The damp grass pricked her toes. Footsteps thumped behind them as sirens wailed down the street. "Stop!" Bobby shouted, as police cars screeched to a halt in front of the house.

Sturdy arms wrapped around Kathy, leading her to safety. Someone yelled at Bobby to drop his gun. A minute later, she watched Bobby stumble toward a police car, his hands helpless behind his back. Just as hers had been only minutes before.

The police took Kathy's statement, and an ambulance carried her and Jack to the hospital. Finally, tucked between the stiff, clean sheets of her bed, she understood that she and Jack were safe. Only then could she take a long, deep breath.

Chapter Seven

The last morning, Kathy phoned Lisa. She felt very thankful that her stepdaughter had slept over at her friend's house. Kathy told Lisa what had happened. "I'll be right there," Lisa said.

In less than twenty minutes, Lisa was at Kathy's bedside. She was crying, her pretty face swollen with tears. Her long, brown hair hung limp past her shoulders to her waist. "How's my dad?" Lisa asked Kathy.

"He's in surgery," Kathy told her. "His nose was broken. And some of his ribs. The doctors might have to take out his spleen."

"Oh, God. Will he be okay?"

"Yes," Kathy said. "He'll be fine. What about you?"

"Me?" Lisa looked surprised by the question. "Nothing happened to me."

"What happened is pretty scary for all of us," Kathy said.

"Were you scared?" Lisa asked.

"Of course."

"It's hard to picture you being scared," Lisa said. "Of anything."

"Are you kidding?" Kathy said. "I'm scared of everything."

Lisa smiled. "Me, too." She reached across the hospital bed and took Kathy's hand in hers. "The nurse told me that the police caught the other guy."

"Good," Kathy said. "I'm glad."

"So, everything will be okay now?" Lisa asked.

"Yes," Kathy told her stepdaughter. "Everything is going to be okay."

Good ∎ Reads

Discover Canada's Bestselling Authors with Good Reads Books

Good Reads authors have a special talent—
the ability to tell a great story, using clear language.

Good Reads books are ideal for people

✳ on the go, who want a short read;
✳ who want to experience the joy of reading;
✳ who want to get into the reading habit.

To find out more, please visit
www.GoodReadsBooks.com

The Good Reads project is sponsored by
ABC Life Literacy Canada.

The project is funded in part by the Government of Canada's
Office of Literacy and Essential Skills.

Libraries and literacy and education markets
order from Grass Roots Press.

Bookstores and other retail outlets order from HarperCollins Canada.

Good Reads Series

If you enjoyed this Good Reads book,
you can find more at your local library or bookstore.

∗

The Stalker by Gail Anderson-Dargatz

In From the Cold by Deborah Ellis

New Year's Eve by Marina Endicott

The Day the Rebels Came to Town by Robert Hough

Picture This by Anthony Hyde

Missing by Frances Itani

Shipwreck by Maureen Jennings

The Picture of Nobody by Rabindranath Maharaj

The Hangman by Louise Penny

Easy Money by Gail Vaz-Oxlade

∗

For more information on Good Reads,
visit **www.GoodReadsBooks.com**

Missing

By Frances Itani

Missing is based on a true story.

Luc Caron lives in northern France during World War I. One day, he sees three airplanes fighting in the sky. Luc watches in horror as a plane flips over and the pilot falls to his death. Luc is the only witness.

The Greenwoods own an apple farm in Canada. Their son, a pilot, has been missing for 11 years. In 1928, they receive a package from England. The package contains a letter and three objects found at the site of a plane crash.

How is the mystery of the missing pilot solved, bringing peace to Luc and to the pilot's parents?

New Year's Eve

By Marina Endicott

On New Year's Eve, Dixie and her husband Grady set off on a car trip. They plan to visit Grady's family, five hours away. But soon they're caught in a blizzard. They turn off the highway and go to their friend Ron's house. Both Grady and Ron are RCMP officers. When Ron must go out on duty, Grady goes with him.

Dixie spends the evening sharing secrets with a couple of other RCMP wives. By midnight, Dixie has learned a thing or two about marriage, and about love.

New Year's Eve leads to a turning point for Dixie and Grady. And a new road for them both.

Picture This

By Anthony Hyde

Paul Stone is an artist. One day, a beautiful woman named Zena walks into his studio. For Paul, it is love at first sight. Zena offers Paul a simple, but strange, job. When Paul takes the job, he steps into a world of trouble.

Zena is mixed up with a crook. They are planning to steal three paintings. Paul finds himself dragged into an art theft worth $3 million. As time goes on, Paul learns he is being lied to, even by Zena. Will Paul stick to the plan? Who will end up with the money? And who will go to jail?

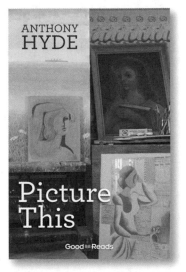

About the Author

Joy Fielding is an internationally bestselling author. Five of her novels have been made into TV movies. She was named Author of the Year in 2005 by the Canada News Group.

Joy worked as an actress before becoming an author. Joy is married and has two daughters and one grandson. She divides her time between Toronto and Palm Beach.

Also by Joy Fielding:

The Other Woman	*Missing Pieces*	*Heartstopper*
Life Penalty	*The First Time*	*Charley's Web*
The Deep End	*Grand Avenue*	*Still Life*
Good Intentions	*Whispers and Lies*	*The Wild Zone*
See Jane Run	*Lost*	*Now You See Her*
Tell Me No Secrets	*Puppet*	
Don't Cry Now	*Mad River Road*	

*

You can visit Joy's website at
www.joyfielding.com